L.&.D
edition

The Prussian Officer

Lawrence, David Herbert

Published: 1914

About Lawrence:

David Herbert Lawrence (11 September 1885 - 2 March 1930) was an English novelist, poet, playwright, essayist, literary critic and painter. His collected works represent, among other things, an extended reflection upon the dehumanising effects of modernity and industrialisation. Some of the issues Lawrence explores are sexuality, emotional health, vitality, spontaneity, and instinct.

Lawrence's opinions earned him many enemies and he endured official persecution, censorship, and misrepresentation of his creative work throughout the second half of his life, much of which he spent in a voluntary exile he called his "savage pilgrimage". At the time of his death, his public reputation was that of a pornographer who had wasted his considerable talents. E. M. Forster, in an obituary notice, challenged this widely held view, describing him as "the greatest imaginative novelist of our generation." Later, Cambridge critic F. R. Leavis championed both his artistic integrity and his moral seriousness, placing much of Lawrence's fiction within the canonical "great tradition" of the English novel.

Chapter 1

They had marched more than thirty kilometres since dawn, along the white, hot road where occasional thickets of trees threw a moment of shade, then out into the glare again. On either hand, the valley, wide and shallow, glittered with heat; dark green patches of rye, pale young corn, fallow and meadow and black pine woods spread in a dull, hot diagram under a glistening sky. But right in front the mountains ranged across, pale blue and very still, snow gleaming gently out of the deep atmosphere. And towards the mountains, on and on, the regiment marched between the rye fields and the meadows, between the scraggy fruit trees set regularly on either side the high road. The burnished, dark green rye threw off a suffocating heat, the mountains drew gradually nearer and more distinct. While the feet of the soldiers grew hotter, sweat ran through their hair under their helmets, and their knapsacks could burn no more in contact with their shoulders, but seemed instead to give off a cold, prickly sensation.

He walked on and on in silence, staring at the mountains ahead, that rose sheer out of the land, and stood fold behind fold, half earth, half heaven, the heaven, the barrier with slits of soft snow, in the pale, bluish peaks.

He could now walk almost without pain. At the start, he had determined not to limp. It had made him sick to take the first steps, and during the first mile or so, he had compressed his breath, and the cold drops of sweat had stood on his forehead. But he had walked it off. What were they after all but bruises! He had looked at them, as he was getting up: deep bruises on the backs of his thighs. And since he had made his first step in the morning, he had been conscious of them, till now he had a tight, hot place in his chest, with suppressing the pain, and holding himself in. There seemed no air when he breathed. But he walked almost lightly.

The Captain's hand had trembled at taking his coffee at dawn: his orderly saw it again. And he saw the fine figure of the Captain wheeling on horseback at the farm-house ahead, a handsome figure in pale blue uniform with facings of scarlet, and the metal gleaming on the black helmet and the sword-scabbard, and dark streaks of sweat coming on the silky bay horse. The orderly felt he was connected with that figure moving so suddenly on horseback: he followed it like a shadow, mute and inevitable and damned by it. And the officer was always aware of the tramp of the company behind, the march of his orderly among the men.

The Captain was a tall man of about forty, grey at the temples. He had a handsome, finely knit figure, and was one of the best horsemen in the West. His orderly, having to rub him down, admired the amazing riding-muscles of his loins.

For the rest, the orderly scarcely noticed the officer any more than he noticed himself. It was rarely he saw his master's face: he did not look at it. The Captain had reddish-brown, stiff hair, that he wore short upon his skull. His moustache was also cut short and bristly over a full, brutal mouth. His face was rather rugged, the cheeks thin. Perhaps the man was the more handsome for the deep lines in his face, the irritable tension of his brow, which gave him the look of a man who fights with life. His fair eyebrows stood bushy over light blue eyes that were always flashing with cold fire.

He was a Prussian aristocrat, haughty and overbearing. But his mother had been a Polish Countess. Having made too many gambling debts when he was young, he had ruined his prospects in the Army, and remained an infantry captain. He had never married: his position did not allow of it, and no woman had ever moved him to it. His time he spent riding—occasionally he rode one of his own horses at the races—and at the officers' club. Now and then he took himself a mistress. But after such an event, he returned to duty with his brow still more tense, his eyes still more hostile and irritable. With the men, however, he was merely impersonal, though a devil when roused; so that, on the whole, they feared him, but had no great aversion from him. They accepted him as the inevitable.

To his orderly he was at first cold and just and indifferent: he did not fuss over trifles. So that his servant knew practically nothing about him, except just what orders he would give, and how he wanted them obeyed. That was quite simple. Then the change gradually came.

The orderly was a youth of about twenty-two, of medium height, and well built. He had strong, heavy limbs, was swarthy, with a soft, black, young moustache. There was something altogether warm and young about him. He had firmly marked eyebrows over dark, expressionless eyes, that seemed never to have thought, only to have received life direct through his senses, and acted straight from instinct.

Gradually the officer had become aware of his servant's young, vigorous, unconscious presence about him. He could not get away from the sense of the youth's person, while he was in attendance. It was like a warm flame upon the older man's tense, rigid body, that had become almost unliving, fixed. There was something so free and self-contained about him, and something in the young fellow's movement, that made the officer aware of him. And this irritated the Prussian. He did not choose to be touched into life by his servant. He might easily have changed his man, but he did not. He now very rarely looked direct at his orderly, but kept his face averted, as if to avoid seeing him. And yet as the young soldier moved unthinking about the apartment, the elder watched him, and would notice the movement of his strong young shoulders under the blue cloth, the bend of his neck. And it irritated him. To see the soldier's young, brown, shapely peasant's hand grasp the loaf or the wine-bottle sent a flash of hate or of anger through the elder man's blood. It was not that the youth was clumsy: it was rather the blind, instinctive sureness of movement of an unhampered young animal that irritated the officer to such a degree.

Once, when a bottle of wine had gone over, and the red gushed out on to the tablecloth, the officer had started up with an oath, and his eyes, bluey like fire, had held those of the confused youth for a moment. It was a shock for the young soldier. He felt something sink deeper, deeper into his soul, where nothing had ever gone before. It left him rather blank and wondering. Some of his natural completeness in himself was gone, a little uneasiness took its place. And from that time an undiscovered feeling had held between the two men.

Henceforward the orderly was afraid of really meeting his master. His subconsciousness remembered those steely blue eyes and the harsh brows, and did not intend to meet them again. So he always stared past his master, and avoided him. Also, in a little anxiety, he waited for the three months to have gone, when his time would be up. He began to feel a constraint in the Captain's presence, and the soldier even more than the officer wanted to be left alone, in his neutrality as servant.

He had served the Captain for more than a year, and knew his duty. This he performed easily, as if it were natural to him. The officer and his commands he took for granted, as he took the sun and the rain, and he served as a matter of course. It did not implicate him personally.

But now if he were going to be forced into a personal interchange with his master he would be like a wild thing caught, he felt he must get away.

But the influence of the young soldier's being had penetrated through the officer's stiffened discipline, and perturbed the man in him. He, however, was a gentleman, with long, fine hands and cultivated movements, and was not going to allow such a thing as the stirring of his innate self. He was a man of passionate temper, who had always kept himself suppressed. Occasionally there had been a duel, an outburst before the soldiers. He knew himself to be always on the point of breaking out. But he kept himself hard to the idea of the Service. Whereas the young soldier seemed to live out his warm, full nature, to give it off in his very movements, which had a certain zest, such as wild animals have in free movement. And this irritated the officer more and more.

In spite of himself, the Captain could not regain his neutrality of feeling towards his orderly. Nor could he leave the man alone. In spite of himself, he watched him, gave him sharp orders, tried to take up as much of his time as possible. Sometimes he flew into a rage with the young soldier, and bullied him. Then the orderly shut himself off, as it were out of earshot, and waited, with sullen, flushed face, for the end of the noise. The words never pierced to his intelligence, he made himself, protectively, impervious to the feelings of his master.

He had a scar on his left thumb, a deep seam going across the knuckle. The officer had long suffered from it, and wanted to do something to it. Still it was there, ugly and brutal on the young, brown hand. At last the Captain's reserve gave way. One day, as the orderly was smoothing out the tablecloth, the officer pinned down his thumb with a pencil, asking:

"How did you come by that?"

The young man winced and drew back at attention.

"A wood axe, Herr Hauptmann," he answered.

The officer waited for further explanation. None came. The orderly went about his duties. The elder man was sullenly angry. His servant avoided him. And the next day he had to use all his will-power to avoid seeing the scarred thumb. He wanted to get hold of it and—A hot flame ran in his blood.

He knew his servant would soon be free, and would be glad. As yet, the soldier had held himself off from the elder man. The Captain grew madly irritable. He could not rest when the soldier was away, and when he was present, he glared at him with tormented eyes. He hated those fine, black brows over the unmeaning, dark eyes, he was infuriated by the free movement of the handsome limbs, which no military discipline could make stiff. And he became harsh and cruelly bullying, using contempt and satire. The young soldier only grew more mute and expressionless.

"What cattle were you bred by, that you can't keep straight eyes? Look me in the eyes when I speak to you."

And the soldier turned his dark eyes to the other's face, but there was no sight in them: he stared with the slightest possible cast, holding back his sight, perceiving the blue of his master's eyes, but receiving no look from them. And the elder man went pale, and his reddish eyebrows twitched. He gave his order, barrenly.

Once he flung a heavy military glove into the young soldier's face. Then he had the satisfaction of seeing the black eyes flare up into his own, like a blaze when straw is thrown on a fire. And he had laughed with a little tremor and a sneer.

But there were only two months more. The youth instinctively tried to keep himself intact: he tried to serve the officer as if the latter were an abstract authority and not a man. All his instinct was to avoid personal contact, even definite hate. But in spite of himself the hate grew, responsive to the officer's passion. However, he put it in the background. When he had left the Army he could dare acknowledge it. By nature he was active, and had many friends. He thought what amazing good fellows they were. But, without knowing it, he was alone. Now this solitariness was intensified. It would carry him through his term. But the officer seemed to be going irritably insane, and the youth was deeply frightened.

The soldier had a sweetheart, a girl from the mountains, independent and primitive. The two walked together, rather silently. He went with her, not to talk, but to have his arm round her, and for the physical contact. This eased him, made it easier for him to ignore the Captain; for he could rest with her held fast against his chest. And she, in some unspoken fashion, was there for him. They loved each other.

The Captain perceived it, and was mad with irritation. He kept the young man engaged all the evenings long, and took pleasure in the dark look that came on his face. Occasionally, the eyes of the two men met, those of the younger sullen and dark, doggedly unalterable, those of the elder sneering with restless contempt.

The officer tried hard not to admit the passion that had got hold of him. He would not know that his feeling for his orderly was anything but that of a man incensed by his stupid, perverse servant. So, keeping quite justified and conventional in his consciousness, he let the other thing run on. His nerves, however, were suffering. At last he slung the end of a belt in his servant's face. When he saw the youth start back, the pain-tears in his eyes and the blood on his mouth, he had felt at once a thrill of deep pleasure and of shame.

But this, he acknowledged to himself, was a thing he had never done before. The fellow was too exasperating. His own nerves must be going to pieces. He went away for some days with a woman.

It was a mockery of pleasure. He simply did not want the woman. But he stayed on for his time. At the end of it, he came back in an agony of irritation, torment, and misery. He rode all the evening, then came straight in to supper. His orderly was out. The officer sat with his long, fine hands lying on the table, perfectly still, and all his blood seemed to be corroding.

At last his servant entered. He watched the strong, easy young figure, the fine eyebrows, the thick black hair. In a week's time the youth had got back his old well-being. The hands of the officer twitched and seemed to be full of mad flame. The young man stood at attention, unmoving, shut off.

The meal went in silence. But the orderly seemed eager. He made a clatter with the dishes.

"Are you in a hurry?" asked the officer, watching the intent, warm face of his servant. The other did not reply.

"Will you answer my question?" said the Captain.

"Yes, sir," replied the orderly, standing with his pile of deep Army plates. The Captain waited, looked at him, then asked again:

"Are you in a hurry?"

"Yes, sir," came the answer, that sent a flash through the listener.

"For what?"

"I was going out, sir."

"I want you this evening."

There was a moment's hesitation. The officer had a curious stiffness of countenance.

"Yes, sir," replied the servant, in his throat.

"I want you tomorrow evening also—in fact, you may consider your evenings occupied, unless I give you leave."

The mouth with the young moustache set close.

"Yes, sir," answered the orderly, loosening his lips for a moment.

He again turned to the door.

"And why have you a piece of pencil in your ear?"

The orderly hesitated, then continued on his way without answering. He set the plates in a pile outside the door, took the stump of pencil from his ear, and put it in his pocket. He had been copying a verse for his sweetheart's birthday card. He returned to finish clearing the table. The officer's eyes were dancing, he had a little, eager smile.

"Why have you a piece of pencil in your ear?" he asked.

The orderly took his hands full of dishes. His master was standing near the great green stove, a little smile on his face, his chin thrust forward. When the young soldier saw him his heart suddenly ran hot. He felt blind. Instead of answering, he turned dazedly to the door. As he was crouching to set down the dishes, he was pitched forward by a kick from behind. The pots went in a stream down the stairs, he clung to the pillar of the banisters. And as he was rising he was kicked heavily again, and again, so that he clung sickly to the post for some moments. His master had gone swiftly into the room and closed the door. The maid-servant downstairs looked up the staircase and made a mocking face at the crockery disaster.

The officer's heart was plunging. He poured himself a glass of wine, part of which he spilled on the floor, and gulped the remainder, leaning against the cool, green stove. He heard his man collecting the dishes from the stairs. Pale, as if intoxicated, he waited. The servant entered again. The Captain's heart gave a pang, as of pleasure, seeing the young fellow bewildered and uncertain on his feet, with pain.

"Schöner!" he said.

The soldier was a little slower in coming to attention.

"Yes, sir!"

The youth stood before him, with pathetic young moustache, and fine eyebrows very distinct on his forehead of dark marble.

"I asked you a question."

"Yes, sir."

The officer's tone bit like acid.

"Why had you a pencil in your ear?"

Again the servant's heart ran hot, and he could not breathe. With dark, strained eyes, he looked at the officer, as if fascinated. And he stood there sturdily planted, unconscious. The withering smile came into the Captain's eyes, and he lifted his foot.

"I—I forgot it—sir," panted the soldier, his dark eyes fixed on the other man's dancing blue ones.

"What was it doing there?"

He saw the young man's breast heaving as he made an effort for words.

"I had been writing."

"Writing what?"

Again the soldier looked up and down. The officer could hear him panting. The smile came into the blue eyes. The soldier worked his dry throat, but could not speak. Suddenly the smile lit like a flame on the officer's face, and a kick came heavily against the orderly's thigh. The youth moved a pace sideways. His face went dead, with two black, staring eyes.

"Well?" said the officer.

The orderly's mouth had gone dry, and his tongue rubbed in it as on dry brown-paper. He worked his throat. The officer raised his foot. The servant went stiff.

"Some poetry, sir," came the crackling, unrecognizable sound of his voice.

"Poetry, what poetry?" asked the Captain, with a sickly smile.

Again there was the working in the throat. The Captain's heart had suddenly gone down heavily, and he stood sick and tired.

"For my girl, sir," he heard the dry, inhuman sound.

"Oh!" he said, turning away. "Clear the table."

"Click!" went the soldier's throat; then again, "click!" and then the half-articulate:

"Yes, sir."

The young soldier was gone, looking old, and walking heavily.

The officer, left alone, held himself rigid, to prevent himself from thinking. His instinct warned him that he must not think. Deep inside him was the intense gratification of his passion, still working powerfully. Then there was a counter-action, a horrible breaking down of something inside him, a whole agony of reaction. He stood there for an hour motionless, a chaos of sensations, but rigid with a will to keep blank his consciousness, to prevent his mind grasping. And he held himself so until the worst of the stress had passed, when he began to drink, drank himself to an intoxication, till he slept obliterated. When he woke in the morning he was shaken to the base of his nature. But he had fought off the realization of what he had done. He had prevented his mind from taking it in, had suppressed it along with his instincts, and the conscious man had nothing to do with it. He felt only as after a bout of intoxication, weak, but the affair itself all dim and not to be recovered. Of the drunkenness of his passion he successfully refused remembrance. And when his orderly appeared with coffee, the officer assumed the same self he had had the morning before. He refused the event of the past night—denied it had ever been— and was successful in his denial. He had not done any such thing— not he himself. Whatever there might be lay at the door of a stupid, insubordinate servant.

The orderly had gone about in a stupor all the evening. He drank some beer because he was parched, but not much, the alcohol made his feeling come back, and he could not bear it. He was dulled, as if nine-tenths of the ordinary man in him were inert. He crawled about disfigured. Still, when he thought of the kicks, he went sick, and when he thought of the threat of more kicking, in the room afterwards, his heart went hot and faint, and he panted, remembering the one that had come. He had been forced to say, "For my girl." He was much too done even to want to cry. His mouth hung slightly open, like an idiot's. He felt vacant, and wasted. So, he wandered at his work, painfully, and very slowly and clumsily, fumbling blindly with the brushes, and finding it difficult, when he sat down, to summon the energy to move again. His limbs, his jaw, were slack and nerveless. But he was very tired. He got to bed at last, and slept inert, relaxed, in a sleep that was rather stupor than slumber, a dead night of stupefaction shot through with gleams of anguish.

In the morning were the manoeuvres. But he woke even before the bugle sounded. The painful ache in his chest, the dryness of his throat, the awful steady feeling of misery made his eyes come awake and dreary at once. He knew, without thinking, what had happened. And he knew that the day had come again, when he must go on with his round. The last bit of darkness was being pushed out of the room. He would have to move his inert body and go on. He was so young, and had known so little trouble, that he was bewildered. He only wished it would stay night, so that he could lie still, covered up by the darkness. And yet nothing would prevent the day from coming, nothing would save him from having to get up and saddle the Captain's horse, and make the Captain's coffee. It was there, inevitable. And then, he thought, it was impossible. Yet they would not leave him free. He must go and take the coffee to the Captain. He was too stunned to understand it. He only knew it was inevitable—inevitable, however long he lay inert.

At last, after heaving at himself, for he seemed to be a mass of inertia, he got up. But he had to force every one of his movements from behind, with his will. He felt lost, and dazed, and helpless. Then he clutched hold of the bed, the pain was so keen. And looking at his thighs, he saw the darker bruises on his swarthy flesh and he knew that, if he pressed one of his fingers on one of the bruises, he should faint. But he did not want to faint—he did not want anybody to know. No one should ever know. It was between him and the Captain. There were only the two people in the world now—himself and the Captain.

Slowly, economically, he got dressed and forced himself to walk. Everything was obscure, except just what he had his hands on. But he managed to get through his work. The very pain revived his dull senses. The worst remained yet. He took the tray and went up to the Captain's room. The officer, pale and heavy, sat at the table. The orderly, as he saluted, felt himself put out of existence. He stood still for a moment submitting to his own nullification—then he gathered himself, seemed to regain himself, and then the Captain began to grow vague, unreal, and the younger soldier's heart beat up. He clung to this situation—that the Captain did not exist—so that he himself might live. But when he saw his officer's hand tremble as he took the coffee, he felt everything falling shattered. And he went away, feeling as if he himself were coming to pieces, disintegrated. And when the Captain was there on horseback, giving orders, while he himself stood, with rifle and knapsack, sick with pain, he felt as if he must shut his eyes—as if he must shut his eyes on everything. It was only the long agony of marching with a parched throat that filled him with one single, sleep-heavy intention: to save himself.

Chapter 2

He was getting used even to his parched throat. That the snowy peaks were radiant among the sky, that the whity-green glacier-river twisted through its pale shoals, in the valley below, seemed almost supernatural. But he was going mad with fever and thirst. He plodded on uncomplaining. He did not want to speak, not to anybody. There were two gulls, like flakes of water and snow, over the river. The scent of green rye soaked in sunshine came like a sickness. And the march continued, monotonously, almost like a bad sleep.

At the next farm-house, which stood low and broad near the high road, tubs of water had been put out. The soldiers clustered round to drink. They took off their helmets, and the steam mounted from their wet hair. The Captain sat on horseback, watching. He needed to see his orderly. His helmet threw a dark shadow over his light, fierce eyes, but his moustache and mouth and chin were distinct in the sunshine. The orderly must move under the presence of the figure of the horseman. It was not that he was afraid, or cowed. It was as if he was disembowelled, made empty, like an empty shell. He felt himself as nothing, a shadow creeping under the sunshine. And, thirsty as he was, he could scarcely drink, feeling the Captain near him. He would not take off his helmet to wipe his wet hair. He wanted to stay in shadow, not to be forced into consciousness. Starting, he saw the light heel of the officer prick the belly of the horse; the Captain cantered away, and he himself could relapse into vacancy.

Nothing, however, could give him back his living place in the hot, bright morning. He felt like a gap among it all. Whereas the Captain was prouder, overriding. A hot flash went through the young servant's body. The Captain was firmer and prouder with life, he himself was empty as a shadow. Again the flash went through him, dazing him out. But his heart ran a little firmer.

The company turned up the hill, to make a loop for the return. Below, from among the trees, the farm-bell clanged. He saw the labourers, mowing barefoot at the thick grass, leave off their work and go downhill, their scythes hanging over their shoulders, like long, bright claws curving down behind them. They seemed like dream-people, as if they had no relation to himself. He felt as in a blackish dream: as if all the other things were there and had form, but he himself was only a consciousness, a gap that could think and perceive.

The soldiers were tramping silently up the glaring hillside. Gradually his head began to revolve, slowly, rhythmically. Sometimes it was dark before his eyes, as if he saw this world through a smoked glass, frail shadows and unreal. It gave him a pain in his head to walk.

The air was too scented, it gave no breath. All the lush greenstuff seemed to be issuing its sap, till the air was deathly, sickly with the smell of greenness. There was the perfume of clover, like pure honey and bees. Then there grew a faint acrid tang—they were near the beeches; and then a queer clattering noise, and a suffocating, hideous smell; they were passing a flock of sheep, a shepherd in a black smock, holding his crook. Why should the sheep huddle together under this fierce sun? He felt that the shepherd would not see him, though he could see the shepherd.

At last there was the halt. They stacked rifles in a conical stack, put down their kit in a scattered circle around it, and dispersed a little, sitting on a small knoll high on the hillside. The chatter began. The soldiers were steaming with heat, but were lively. He sat still, seeing the blue mountains rising upon the land, twenty kilometres away. There was a blue fold in the ranges, then out of that, at the foot, the broad, pale bed of the river, stretches of whity-green water between pinkish-grey shoals among the dark pine woods. There it was, spread out a long way off. And it seemed to come downhill, the river. There was a raft being steered, a mile away. It was a strange country. Nearer, a red-roofed, broad farm with white base and square dots of windows crouched beside the wall of beech foliage on the wood's edge. There were long strips of rye and clover and pale green corn. And just at his feet, below the knoll, was a darkish bog, where globe flowers stood breathless still on their slim stalks. And some of the pale gold bubbles were burst, and a broken fragment hung in the air. He thought he was going to sleep.

Suddenly something moved into this coloured mirage before his eyes. The Captain, a small, light-blue and scarlet figure, was trotting evenly between the strips of corn, along the level brow of the hill. And the man making flag-signals was coming on. Proud and sure moved the horseman's figure, the quick, bright thing, in which was concentrated all the light of this morning, which for the rest lay a fragile, shining shadow. Submissive, apathetic, the young soldier sat and stared. But as the horse slowed to a walk, coming up the last steep path, the great flash flared over the body and soul of the orderly. He sat waiting. The back of his head felt as if it were weighted with a heavy piece of fire. He did not want to eat. His hands trembled slightly as he moved them. Meanwhile the officer on horseback was approaching slowly and proudly. The tension grew in the orderly's soul. Then again, seeing the Captain ease himself on the saddle, the flash blazed through him.

The Captain looked at the patch of light blue and scarlet, and dark heads, scattered closely on the hillside. It pleased him. The command pleased him. And he was feeling proud. His orderly was among them in common subjection. The officer rose a little on his stirrups to look. The young soldier sat with averted, dumb face. The Captain relaxed on his seat. His slim-legged, beautiful horse, brown as a beech nut, walked proudly uphill. The Captain passed into the zone of the company's atmosphere: a hot smell of men, of sweat, of leather. He knew it very well. After a word with the lieutenant, he went a few paces higher, and sat there, a dominant figure, his sweat-marked horse swishing its tail, while he looked down on his men, on his orderly, a nonentity among the crowd.

The young soldier's heart was like fire in his chest, and he breathed with difficulty. The officer, looking downhill, saw three of the young soldiers, two pails of water between them, staggering across a sunny green field. A table had been set up under a tree, and there the slim lieutenant stood, importantly busy. Then the Captain summoned himself to an act of courage. He called his orderly.

The flame leapt into the young soldier's throat as he heard the command, and he rose blindly, stifled. He saluted, standing below the officer. He did not look up. But there was the flicker in the Captain's voice.

"Go to the inn and fetch me ... " the officer gave his commands. "Quick!" he added.

At the last word, the heart of the servant leapt with a flash, and he felt the strength come over his body. But he turned in mechanical obedience, and set off at a heavy run downhill, looking almost like a bear, his trousers bagging over his military boots. And the officer watched this blind, plunging run all the way.

But it was only the outside of the orderly's body that was obeying so humbly and mechanically. Inside had gradually accumulated a core into which all the energy of that young life was compact and concentrated. He executed his commission, and plodded quickly back uphill. There was a pain in his head, as he walked, that made him twist his features unknowingly. But hard there in the centre of his chest was himself, himself, firm, and not to be plucked to pieces.

The Captain had gone up into the wood. The orderly plodded through the hot, powerfully smelling zone of the company's atmosphere. He had a curious mass of energy inside him now. The Captain was less real than himself. He approached the green entrance to the wood. There, in the half-shade, he saw the horse standing, the sunshine and the flickering shadow of leaves dancing over his brown body. There was a clearing where timber had lately been felled. Here, in the gold-green shade beside the brilliant cup of sunshine, stood two figures, blue and pink, the bits of pink showing out plainly. The Captain was talking to his lieutenant.

The orderly stood on the edge of the bright clearing, where great trunks of trees, stripped and glistening, lay stretched like naked, brown-skinned bodies. Chips of wood littered the trampled floor, like splashed light, and the bases of the felled trees stood here and there, with their raw, level tops. Beyond was the brilliant, sunlit green of a beech.

"Then I will ride forward," the orderly heard his Captain say. The lieutenant saluted and strode away. He himself went forward. A hot flash passed through his belly, as he tramped towards his officer.

The Captain watched the rather heavy figure of the young soldier stumble forward, and his veins, too, ran hot. This was to be man to man between them. He yielded before the solid, stumbling figure with bent head. The orderly stooped and put the food on a level-sawn tree-base. The Captain watched the glistening, sun-inflamed, naked hands. He wanted to speak to the young soldier, but could not. The servant propped a bottle against his thigh, pressed open the cork, and poured out the beer into the mug. He kept his head bent. The Captain accepted the mug.

"Hot!" he said, as if amiably.

The flame sprang out of the orderly's heart, nearly suffocating him.

"Yes, sir," he replied, between shut teeth.

And he heard the sound of the Captain's drinking, and he clenched his fists, such a strong torment came into his wrists. Then came the faint clang of the closing pot-lid. He looked up. The Captain was watching him. He glanced swiftly away. Then he saw the officer stoop and take a piece of bread from the tree-base. Again the flash of flame went through the young soldier, seeing the stiff body stoop beneath him, and his hands jerked. He looked away. He could feel the officer was nervous. The bread fell as it was being broken. The officer ate the other piece. The two men stood tense and still, the master laboriously chewing his bread, the servant staring with averted face, his fist clenched.

Then the young soldier started. The officer had pressed open the lid of the mug again. The orderly watched the lid of the mug, and the white hand that clenched the handle, as if he were fascinated. It was raised. The youth followed it with his eyes. And then he saw the thin, strong throat of the elder man moving up and down as he drank, the strong jaw working. And the instinct which had been jerking at the young man's wrists suddenly jerked free. He jumped, feeling as if it were rent in two by a strong flame.

The spur of the officer caught in a tree-root, he went down backwards with a crash, the middle of his back thudding sickeningly against a sharp-edged tree-base, the pot flying away. And in a second the orderly, with serious, earnest young face, and underlip between his teeth, had got his knee in the officer's chest and was pressing the chin backward over the farther edge of the tree-stump, pressing, with all his heart behind in a passion of relief, the tension of his wrists exquisite with relief. And with the base of his palms he shoved at the chin, with all his might. And it was pleasant, too, to have that chin, that hard jaw already slightly rough with beard, in his hands. He did not relax one hair's breadth, but, all the force of all his blood exulting in his thrust, he shoved back the head of the other man, till there was a little "cluck" and a crunching sensation. Then he felt as if his head went to vapour. Heavy convulsions shook the body of the officer, frightening and horrifying the young soldier. Yet it pleased him, too, to repress them. It pleased him to keep his hands pressing back the chin, to feel the chest of the other man yield in expiration to the weight of his strong, young knees, to feel the hard twitchings of the prostrate body jerking his own whole frame, which was pressed down on it.

But it went still. He could look into the nostrils of the other man, the eyes he could scarcely see. How curiously the mouth was pushed out, exaggerating the full lips, and the moustache bristling up from them. Then, with a start, he noticed the nostrils gradually filled with blood. The red brimmed, hesitated, ran over, and went in a thin trickle down the face to the eyes.

It shocked and distressed him. Slowly, he got up. The body twitched and sprawled there, inert. He stood and looked at it in silence. It was a pity IT was broken. It represented more than the thing which had kicked and bullied him. He was afraid to look at the eyes. They were hideous now, only the whites showing, and the blood running to them. The face of the orderly was drawn with horror at the sight. Well, it was so. In his heart he was satisfied. He had hated the face of the Captain. It was extinguished now. There was a heavy relief in the orderly's soul. That was as it should be. But he could not bear to see the long, military body lying broken over the tree-base, the fine fingers crisped. He wanted to hide it away.

Quickly, busily, he gathered it up and pushed it under the felled tree-trunks, which rested their beautiful, smooth length either end on logs. The face was horrible with blood. He covered it with the helmet. Then he pushed the limbs straight and decent, and brushed the dead leaves off the fine cloth of the uniform. So, it lay quite still in the shadow under there. A little strip of sunshine ran along the breast, from a chink between the logs. The orderly sat by it for a few moments. Here his own life also ended.

Then, through his daze, he heard the lieutenant, in a loud voice, explaining to the men outside the wood, that they were to suppose the bridge on the river below was held by the enemy. Now they were to march to the attack in such and such a manner. The lieutenant had no gift of expression. The orderly, listening from habit, got muddled. And when the lieutenant began it all again he ceased to hear.

He knew he must go. He stood up. It surprised him that the leaves were glittering in the sun, and the chips of wood reflecting white from the ground. For him a change had come over the world. But for the rest it had not—all seemed the same. Only he had left it. And he could not go back. It was his duty to return with the beer-pot and the bottle. He could not. He had left all that. The lieutenant was still hoarsely explaining. He must go, or they would overtake him. And he could not bear contact with anyone now.

He drew his fingers over his eyes, trying to find out where he was. Then he turned away. He saw the horse standing in the path. He went up to it and mounted. It hurt him to sit in the saddle. The pain of keeping his seat occupied him as they cantered through the wood. He would not have minded anything, but he could not get away from the sense of being divided from the others. The path led out of the trees. On the edge of the wood he pulled up and stood watching. There in the spacious sunshine of the valley soldiers were moving in a little swarm. Every now and then, a man harrowing on a strip of fallow shouted to his oxen, at the turn. The village and the white-towered church was small in the sunshine. And he no longer belonged to it—he sat there, beyond, like a man outside in the dark. He had gone out from everyday life into the unknown, and he could not, he even did not want to go back.

Turning from the sun-blazing valley, he rode deep into the wood. Tree-trunks, like people standing grey and still, took no notice as he went. A doe, herself a moving bit of sunshine and shadow, went running through the flecked shade. There were bright green rents in the foliage. Then it was all pine wood, dark and cool. And he was sick with pain, he had an intolerable great pulse in his head, and he was sick. He had never been ill in his life. He felt lost, quite dazed with all this.

Trying to get down from the horse, he fell, astonished at the pain and his lack of balance. The horse shifted uneasily. He jerked its bridle and sent it cantering jerkily away. It was his last connection with the rest of things.

But he only wanted to lie down and not be disturbed. Stumbling through the trees, he came on a quiet place where beeches and pine trees grew on a slope. Immediately he had lain down and closed his eyes, his consciousness went racing on without him. A big pulse of sickness beat in him as if it throbbed through the whole earth. He was burning with dry heat. But he was too busy, too tearingly active in the incoherent race of delirium to observe.

Chapter 3

He came to with a start. His mouth was dry and hard, his heart beat heavily, but he had not the energy to get up. His heart beat heavily. Where was he?—the barracks—at home? There was something knocking. And, making an effort, he looked round—trees, and litter of greenery, and reddish, bright, still pieces of sunshine on the floor. He did not believe he was himself, he did not believe what he saw. Something was knocking. He made a struggle towards consciousness, but relapsed. Then he struggled again. And gradually his surroundings fell into relationship with himself. He knew, and a great pang of fear went through his heart. Somebody was knocking. He could see the heavy, black rags of a fir tree overhead. Then everything went black. Yet he did not believe he had closed his eyes. He had not. Out of the blackness sight slowly emerged again. And someone was knocking. Quickly, he saw the blood-disfigured face of his Captain, which he hated. And he held himself still with horror. Yet, deep inside him, he knew that it was so, the Captain should be dead. But the physical delirium got hold of him. Someone was knocking. He lay perfectly still, as if dead, with fear. And he went unconscious.

When he opened his eyes again, he started, seeing something creeping swiftly up a tree-trunk. It was a little bird. And the bird was whistling overhead. Tap-tap-tap—it was the small, quick bird rapping the tree-trunk with its beak, as if its head were a little round hammer. He watched it curiously. It shifted sharply, in its creeping fashion. Then, like a mouse, it slid down the bare trunk. Its swift creeping sent a flash of revulsion through him. He raised his head. It felt a great weight. Then, the little bird ran out of the shadow across a still patch of sunshine, its little head bobbing swiftly, its white legs twinkling brightly for a moment. How neat it was in its build, so compact, with pieces of white on its wings. There were several of them. They were so pretty—but they crept like swift, erratic mice, running here and there among the beech-mast.

He lay down again exhausted, and his consciousness lapsed. He had a horror of the little creeping birds. All his blood seemed to be darting and creeping in his head. And yet he could not move.

He came to with a further ache of exhaustion. There was the pain in his head, and the horrible sickness, and his inability to move. He had never been ill in his life. He did not know where he was or what he was. Probably he had got sunstroke. Or what else?—he had silenced the Captain for ever—some time ago—oh, a long time ago. There had been blood on his face, and his eyes had turned upwards. It was all right, somehow. It was peace. But now he had got beyond himself. He had never been here before. Was it life, or not life? He was by himself. They were in a big, bright place, those others, and he was outside. The town, all the country, a big bright place of light: and he was outside, here, in the darkened open beyond, where each thing existed alone. But they would all have to come out there sometime, those others. Little, and left behind him, they all were. There had been father and mother and sweetheart. What did they all matter? This was the open land.

He sat up. Something scuffled. It was a little, brown squirrel running in lovely, undulating bounds over the floor, its red tail completing the undulation of its body—and then, as it sat up, furling and unfurling. He watched it, pleased. It ran on again, friskily, enjoying itself. It flew wildly at another squirrel, and they were chasing each other, and making little scolding, chattering noises. The soldier wanted to speak to them. But only a hoarse sound came out of his throat. The squirrels burst away— they flew up the trees. And then he saw the one peeping round at him, half-way up a tree-trunk. A start of fear went through him, though, in so far as he was conscious, he was amused. It still stayed, its little, keen face staring at him halfway up the tree-trunk, its little ears pricked up, its clawey little hands clinging to the bark, its white breast reared. He started from it in panic.

Struggling to his feet, he lurched away. He went on walking, walking, looking for something—for a drink. His brain felt hot and inflamed for want of water. He stumbled on. Then he did not know anything. He went unconscious as he walked. Yet he stumbled on, his mouth open.

When, to his dumb wonder, he opened his eyes on the world again, he no longer tried to remember what it was. There was thick, golden light behind golden-green glitterings, and tall, grey-purple shafts, and darknesses further off, surrounding him, growing deeper. He was conscious of a sense of arrival. He was amid the reality, on the real, dark bottom. But there was the thirst burning in his brain. He felt lighter, not so heavy. He supposed it was newness. The air was muttering with thunder. He thought he was walking wonderfully swiftly and was coming straight to relief— or was it to water?

Suddenly he stood still with fear. There was a tremendous flare of gold, immense—just a few dark trunks like bars between him and it. All the young level wheat was burnished gold glaring on its silky green. A woman, full-skirted, a black cloth on her head for head-dress, was passing like a block of shadow through the glistening, green corn, into the full glare. There was a farm, too, pale blue in shadow, and the timber black. And there was a church spire, nearly fused away in the gold. The woman moved on, away from him. He had no language with which to speak to her. She was the bright, solid unreality. She would make a noise of words that would confuse him, and her eyes would look at him without seeing him. She was crossing there to the other side. He stood against a tree.

When at last he turned, looking down the long, bare grove whose flat bed was already filling dark, he saw the mountains in a wonder-light, not far away, and radiant. Behind the soft, grey ridge of the nearest range the further mountains stood golden and pale grey, the snow all radiant like pure, soft gold. So still, gleaming in the sky, fashioned pure out of the ore of the sky, they shone in their silence. He stood and looked at them, his face illuminated. And like the golden, lustrous gleaming of the snow he felt his own thirst bright in him. He stood and gazed, leaning against a tree. And then everything slid away into space.

During the night the lightning fluttered perpetually, making the whole sky white. He must have walked again. The world hung livid round him for moments, fields a level sheen of grey-green light, trees in dark bulk, and the range of clouds black across a white sky. Then the darkness fell like a shutter, and the night was whole. A faint flutter of a half-revealed world, that could not quite leap out of the darkness!—Then there again stood a sweep of pallor for the land, dark shapes looming, a range of clouds hanging overhead. The world was a ghostly shadow, thrown for a moment upon the pure darkness, which returned ever whole and complete.

And the mere delirium of sickness and fever went on inside him— his brain opening and shutting like the night—then sometimes convulsions of terror from something with great eyes that stared round a tree—then the long agony of the march, and the sun decomposing his blood—then the pang of hate for the Captain, followed by a pang of tenderness and ease. But everything was distorted, born of an ache and resolving into an ache.

In the morning he came definitely awake. Then his brain flamed with the sole horror of thirstiness! The sun was on his face, the dew was steaming from his wet clothes. Like one possessed, he got up. There, straight in front of him, blue and cool and tender, the mountains ranged across the pale edge of the morning sky. He wanted them—he wanted them alone—he wanted to leave himself and be identified with them. They did not move, they were still soft, with white, gentle markings of snow. He stood still, mad with suffering, his hands crisping and clutching. Then he was twisting in a paroxysm on the grass.

He lay still, in a kind of dream of anguish. His thirst seemed to have separated itself from him, and to stand apart, a single demand. Then the pain he felt was another single self. Then there was the clog of his body, another separate thing. He was divided among all kinds of separate beings. There was some strange, agonized connection between them, but they were drawing further apart. Then they would all split. The sun, drilling down on him, was drilling through the bond. Then they would all fall, fall through the everlasting lapse of space. Then again, his consciousness reasserted itself. He roused on to his elbow and stared at the gleaming mountains. There they ranked, all still and wonderful between earth and heaven. He stared till his eyes went black, and the mountains, as they stood in their beauty, so clean and cool, seemed to have it, that which was lost in him.

Chapter 4

When the soldiers found him, three hours later, he was lying with his face over his arm, his black hair giving off heat under the sun. But he was still alive. Seeing the open, black mouth the young soldiers dropped him in horror.

He died in the hospital at night, without having seen again.

The doctors saw the bruises on his legs, behind, and were silent.

The bodies of the two men lay together, side by side, in the mortuary, the one white and slender, but laid rigidly at rest, the other looking as if every moment it must rouse into life again, so young and unused, from a slumber.

Biography & Bibliographiy

David Herbert Lawrence

David Herbert Lawrence (11 September 1885 - 2 March 1930) was an English novelist, poet, playwright, essayist, literary critic and painter. His collected works represent, among other things, an extended reflection upon the dehumanising effects of modernity and industrialisation. Some of the issues Lawrence explores are sexuality, emotional health, vitality, spontaneity, and instinct.

Lawrence's opinions earned him many enemies and he endured official persecution, censorship, and misrepresentation of his creative work throughout the second half of his life, much of which he spent in a voluntary exile he called his "savage pilgrimage". At the time of his death, his public reputation was that of a pornographer who had wasted his considerable talents. E. M. Forster, in an obituary notice, challenged this widely held view, describing him as "the greatest imaginative novelist of our generation." Later, Cambridge critic F. R. Leavis championed both his artistic integrity and his moral seriousness, placing much of Lawrence's fiction within the canonical "great tradition" of the English novel.

Life and career

Early life

The fourth child of Arthur John Lawrence, a barely-literate miner at Brinsley Colliery, and Lydia Beardsall, a former pupil teacher who had been forced to perform manual work in a lace factory due to her family's financial difficulties, Lawrence spent his formative years in the coal mining town of Eastwood, Nottinghamshire. The house in which he was born, 8a Victoria Street, is now the D. H. Lawrence Birthplace Museum. His working-class background and the tensions between his parents provided the raw material for a number of his early works. Lawrence roamed out from an early age in the patches of open, hilly country and remaining fragments of Sherwood Forest in Felley woods to the north of Eastwood, beginning a lifelong appreciation of the natural world, and he often wrote about "the country of my heart" as a setting for much of his fiction.

The young Lawrence attended Beauvale Board School (now renamed Greasley Beauvale D. H. Lawrence Primary School in his honour) from 1891 until 1898, becoming the first local pupil to win a County Council scholarship to Nottingham High School in nearby Nottingham. He left in 1901, working for three months as a junior clerk at Haywood's surgical appliances factory, but a severe bout of pneumonia ended this career. During his convalescence he often visited Hagg's Farm, the home of the Chambers family, and began a friendship with Jessie Chambers. An important aspect of this relationship with Chambers and other adolescent acquaintances was a shared love of books, an interest that lasted throughout Lawrence's life. In the years 1902 to 1906 Lawrence served as a pupil teacher at the British School, Eastwood. He went on to become a full-time student and received a teaching certificate from University College, Nottingham, in 1908. During these early years he was working on his first poems, some short stories, and a draft of a novel, Laetitia, which was eventually to become The White Peacock. At the end of 1907 he won a short story competition in the Nottingham Guardian, the first time that he had gained any wider recognition for his literary talents.

Early career

In the autumn of 1908 the newly qualified Lawrence left his childhood home for London. While teaching in Davidson Road School, Croydon, he continued writing. Jessie Chambers submitted some of Lawrence's early poetry to Ford Madox Ford (then known as Ford Hermann Hueffer), editor of the influential The English Review. Hueffer then commissioned the story Odour of Chrysanthemums which, when published in that magazine, encouraged Heinemann, a London publisher, to ask Lawrence for more work. His career as a professional author now began in earnest, although he taught for another year. Shortly after the final proofs of his first published novel, The White Peacock, appeared in 1910, Lawrence's mother died of cancer. The young man was devastated, and he was to describe the next few months as his "sick year". It is clear that Lawrence had an extremely close relationship with his mother, and his grief became a major turning point in his life, just as the death of Mrs. Morel is a major turning point in his autobiographical novel Sons and Lovers, a work that draws upon much of the writer's provincial upbringing. Essentially concerned with the emotional battle for Lawrence's love between his mother and "Miriam" (in reality Jessie Chambers), the novel also documents Paul's (Lawrence's) brief intimate relationship with Miriam (Jessie) that Lawrence had finally initiated in the Christmas of 1909, ending it in August 1910. The hurt caused to Jessie by this and finally by her portrayal in the novel caused the end of their friendship and after it was published they never spoke to each other again.

In 1911 Lawrence was introduced to Edward Garnett, a publisher's reader, who acted as a mentor, provided further encouragement, and became a valued friend, as did his son David. Throughout these months the young author revised Paul Morel, the first draft of what became Sons and Lovers. In addition, a teaching colleague, Helen Corke, gave him access to her intimate diaries about an unhappy love affair, which formed the basis of The Trespasser, his second novel. In November 1911, he came down with a pneumonia again; once he recovered, Lawrence decided to abandon teaching in order to become a full-time writer. He also broke off an engagement to Louie Burrows, an old friend from his days in Nottingham and Eastwood.

In March 1912 Lawrence met Frieda Weekley (née von Richthofen), with whom he was to share the rest of his life. Six years older than her new lover, she was married to Ernest Weekley, his former modern languages professor at University College, Nottingham, and had three young children. She eloped with Lawrence to her parents' home in Metz, a garrison town then in Germany near the disputed border with France. Their stay there included Lawrence's first encounter with tensions between Germany and France, when he was arrested and accused of being a British spy, before being released following an intervention from Frieda's father. After this incident, Lawrence left for a small hamlet to the south of Munich, where he was joined by Frieda for their "honeymoon", later memorialised in the series of love poems titled Look! We Have Come Through (1917). 1912 also saw the first of Lawrence's so-called "mining plays", The Daughter-in-Law, written in Nottingham dialect. The play was never to be performed, or even published, in Lawrence's lifetime.

From Germany they walked southwards across the Alps to Italy, a journey that was recorded in the first of his travel books, a collection of linked essays titled Twilight in Italy and the unfinished novel, Mr Noon. During his stay in Italy, Lawrence completed the final version of Sons and Lovers that, when published in 1913, was acknowledged to be a vivid portrait of the realities of working class provincial life. Lawrence, though, had become so tired of the work that he allowed Edward Garnett to cut about a hundred pages from the text.

Lawrence and Frieda returned to Britain in 1913 for a short visit, during which they encountered and befriended critic John Middleton Murry and New Zealand-born short story writer Katherine Mansfield. Lawrence was able to meet Welsh tramp poet W. H. Davies, whose work, much of which was inspired by nature, he greatly admired. Davies collected autographs, and was particularly keen to obtain Lawrence's. Georgian poetry publisher Edward Marsh was able to secure an autograph (probably as part of a signed poem), and invited Lawrence and Frieda to meet Davies in London on 28 July, under his supervision. Lawrence was immediately captivated by the poet and later invited Davies to join Frieda and himself in Germany. Despite his early enthusiasm for Davies' work, however, Lawrence's opinion changed after reading Foliage and he commented after reading Nature Poems in Italy that they seemed ".. so thin, one can hardly feel them".

Lawrence and Frieda soon went back to Italy, staying in a cottage in Fiascherino on the Gulf of Spezia. Here he started writing the first draft of a work of fiction that was to be transformed into two of his best-known novels, The Rainbow and Women in Love, in which unconventional female characters take centre stage. Both novels were highly controversial, and both were banned on publication in the UK for obscenity (Women in Love only temporarily). Both novels cover grand themes and ideas.

The Rainbow follows three generations of a Nottinghamshire farming family from the pre-industrial to the industrial age, focusing particularly on a daughter, Ursula, and her aspiration for a more fulfilling life than that of becoming a housebound wife. Women in Love delves into the complex relationships between four major characters, including the sisters Ursula and Gudrun. Both novels challenged conventional ideas about the arts, politics, economic growth, gender, sexual experience, friendship and marriage and can be seen as far ahead of their time. The frank and relatively straightforward manner in which Lawrence dealt with sexual attraction was ostensibly what got the books banned, perhaps in particular the mention of same-sex attraction – Ursula has an affair with a woman in The Rainbow and in Women in Love there is an undercurrent of attraction between the two principal male characters.

While writing Women in Love in Cornwall during 1916–17, Lawrence developed a strong and possibly romantic relationship with a Cornish farmer named William Henry Hocking. Although it is not clear if their relationship was sexual, Frieda said she believed it was. Lawrence's fascination with the theme of homosexuality, which is overtly manifested in Women in Love, could be related to his own sexual orientation. In a letter written during 1913, he writes, "I should like to know why nearly every man that approaches greatness tends to homosexuality, whether he admits it or not ..." He is also quoted as saying, "I believe the nearest I've come to perfect love was with a young coal-miner when I was about 16." However, given his enduring and robust relationship with Frieda it is likely that he was primarily "bi-curious" in the terminology of today, and whether he actually ever had homosexual relations remains an open question.

Eventually, Frieda obtained her divorce. The couple returned to Britain shortly before the outbreak of World War I and were married on 13 July 1914. At this time, Lawrence worked with London intellectuals and writers such as Dora Marsden and the people involved with The Egoist (T. S. Eliot, Ezra Pound, and others). The Egoist, an important Modernist literary magazine, published some of his work. He was also reading and adapting Marinetti's Manifesto of Futurism. He also met at this time the young Jewish artist Mark Gertler, and they became (for a time) good friends; Lawrence would describe Gertler's 1916 anti-war painting, Merry-Go-Roundas "the best modern picture I have seen: I think it is great and true." Gertler would inspire the character Loerke (a sculptor) in Women in Love. Frieda's German parentage and Lawrence's open contempt for militarism caused them to be viewed with suspicion in wartime Britain and to live in near destitution. The Rainbow (1915) was suppressed after an investigation into its alleged obscenity in 1915. Later, they were accused of spying and signaling to German submarines off the coast of Cornwall where they lived at Zennor. During this period he finished writing Women in Love. Not published until 1920, it is now widely recognised as an English novel of great dramatic force and intellectual subtlety.

In late 1917, after constant harassment by the armed forces authorities, Lawrence was forced to leave Cornwall at three days' notice under the terms of the Defence of the Realm Act. This persecution was later described in an autobiographical chapter of his Australian novel Kangaroo, published in 1923. He spent some months in early 1918 in the small, rural village of Hermitage near Newbury, Berkshire. He then lived for just under a year (mid-1918 to early 1919) at Mountain Cottage, Middleton-by-Wirksworth, Derbyshire, where he wrote one of his most poetic short stories, Wintry Peacock. Until 1919 he was compelled by poverty to shift from address to address and barely survived a severe attack of influenza.

Exile

After the traumatic experience of the war years, Lawrence began what he termed his "savage pilgrimage", a time of voluntary exile. He escaped from Britain at the earliest practical opportunity, to return only twice for brief visits, and with his wife spent the remainder of his life travelling. This wanderlust took him to Australia, Italy, Ceylon (now called Sri Lanka), the United States, Mexico and the South of France.

Lawrence abandoned Britain in November 1919 and headed south, first to the Abruzzo region in central Italy and then onwards to Capri and the Fontana Vecchia in Taormina, Sicily. From Sicily he made brief excursions to Sardinia, Monte Cassino, Malta, Northern Italy, Austria and Southern Germany. Many of these places appeared in his writings. New novels included The Lost Girl (for which he won the James Tait Black Memorial Prizefor fiction), Aaron's Rod and the fragment titled Mr Noon (the first part of which was published in the Phoenix anthology of his works, and the entirety in 1984). He experimented with shorter novels or novellas, such as The Captain's Doll, The Fox and The Ladybird. In addition, some of his short stories were issued in the collection England, My England and Other Stories. During these years he produced a number of poems about the natural world in Birds, Beasts and Flowers. Lawrence is widely recognised as one of the finest travel writers in the English language. Sea and Sardinia, a book that describes a brief journey undertaken in January 1921, is a recreation of the life of the inhabitants of Sardinia. Less well known is the memoir of Maurice Magnus, Memoirs of the Foreign Legion, in which Lawrence recalls his visit to the monastery of Monte Cassino. Other non-fiction books include two responses to Freudian psychoanalysis and Movements in European History, a school textbook that was published under a pseudonym, a reflection of his blighted reputation in Britain.

Later life and career

In late February 1922 the Lawrences left Europe behind with the intention of migrating to the United States. They sailed in an easterly direction, first to Ceylon and then on to Australia. A short residence in Darlington, Western Australia, which included an encounter with local writer Mollie Skinner, was followed by a brief stop in the small coastal town of Thirroul, New South Wales, during which Lawrence completed Kangaroo, a novel about local fringe politics that also revealed a lot about his wartime experiences in Cornwall.

The Lawrences finally arrived in the US in September 1922. Lawrence had several times discussed the idea of setting up a utopian community with several of his friends, having written to his old socialist friend in Eastwood, Willie Hopkin, in 1915,

> "I want to gather together about twenty souls and sail away from this world of war and squalor and found a little colony where there shall be no money but a sort of communism as far as necessaries of life go, and some real decency... a place where one can live simply, apart from this civilisation... [with] a few other people who are also at peace and happy and live, and understand and be free..."

It was with this in mind that they made for the "bohemian" town of Taos, New Mexico, where Mabel Dodge Luhan, a prominent socialite, lived. Here they eventually acquired the 160-acre (0.65 km2) Kiowa Ranch, now called the D. H. Lawrence Ranch, in 1924 from Dodge Luhan in exchange for the manuscript of Sons and Lovers. He stayed in New Mexico for two years, with extended visits to Lake Chapala and Oaxaca in Mexico. While Lawrence was in New Mexico, he was visited by Aldous Huxley.

While in the U.S., Lawrence rewrote and published Studies in Classic American Literature, a set of critical essays begun in 1917, and later described by Edmund Wilson as "one of the few first-rate books that have ever been written on the subject". These interpretations, with their insights into symbolism, New England Transcendentalism and the puritan sensibility, were a significant factor in the revival of the reputation of Herman Melville during the early 1920s. In addition, Lawrence completed a number of new fictional works, including The Boy in the Bush, The Plumed Serpent, St Mawr, The Woman who Rode Away, The Princess and assorted short stories. He also found time to produce some more travel writing, such as the collection of linked excursions that became Mornings in Mexico.

A brief voyage to England at the end of 1923 was a failure and he soon returned to Taos, convinced that his life as an author now lay in the United States. However, in March 1925 he suffered a near fatal attack of malaria and tuberculosis while on a third visit to Mexico. Although he eventually recovered, the diagnosis of his condition obliged him to return once again to Europe. He was dangerously ill and the poor health limited his ability to travel for the remainder of his life. The Lawrences made their home in a villa in Northern Italy, living near Florence while he wrote The Virgin and the Gipsy and the various versions of Lady Chatterley's Lover(1928). The latter book, his last major novel, was initially published in private editions in Florence and Paris and reinforced his notoriety. A story set once more in Nottinghamshire about a cross-class relationship between a Lady and her gamekeeper, it broke new ground in describing their sexual relationship in explicit yet literary language. His intention in writing the novel was to challenge the British establishment's taboos around sex, to enable men and women "...to think sex, fully, completely, honestly, and cleanly." Lawrence responded robustly to those who claimed to be offended, penning a large number of satirical poems, published under the title of "Pansies" and "Nettles", as well as a tract on Pornography and Obscenity.

The return to Italy allowed Lawrence to renew old friendships; during these years he was particularly close to Aldous Huxley, who was to edit the first collection of Lawrence's letters after his death, along with a memoir. With artist Earl Brewster, Lawrence visited a number of local archaeological sites in April 1927. The resulting essays describing these visits to old tombs were written up and collected together as Sketches of Etruscan Places, a book that contrasts the lively past with Benito Mussolini's fascism. Lawrence continued to produce fiction, including short stories and The Escaped Cock (also published as The Man Who Died), an unorthodox reworking of the story of Jesus Christ's Resurrection. During these final years Lawrence renewed a serious interest in oil painting. Official harassment persisted and an exhibition of some of these pictures at the Warren Gallery in London was raided by the police in mid 1929 and a number of works were confiscated.

Death

Lawrence continued to write despite his failing health. In his last months he wrote numerous poems, reviews and essays, as well as a robust defence of his last novel against those who sought to suppress it. His last significant work was a reflection on the Book of Revelation, Apocalypse. After being discharged from a sanatorium, he died on 2 March 1930 at the Villa Robermond in Vence, France, from complications of tuberculosis. Frieda Weekley commissioned an elaborate headstone for his grave bearing a mosaic of his adopted emblem of the phoenix. After Lawrence's death, Frieda lived with Angelo Ravagli on the ranch in Taos and eventually married him in 1950. In 1935 Ravagli arranged, on Frieda's behalf, to have Lawrence's body exhumed and cremated and his ashes brought back to the ranch to be interred there in a small chapel amid the mountains of New Mexico.

Philosophy and politics

Critic Terry Eagleton situates Lawrence on the radical right wing of politics, as hostile to democracy, liberalism, socialism, and egalitarianism, though never formally embracing fascism, as he died before it reached its zenith. Lawrence's opinion of the masses is discussed in detail by Professor John Carey in The Intellectuals and the Masses (1992), and he quotes a 1908 letter from Lawrence to Blanche Jennings:

> If I had my way, I would build a lethal chamber as big as the Crystal Palace, with a military band playing softly, and a Cinematograph working brightly ; then I'd go out in the back streets and main streets and bring them in, all the sick, the halt, and the maimed ; I would lead them gently, and they would smile me a weary thanks ; and the band would softly bubble out the "Hallelujah Chorus".

More of Lawrence's political ideas can be seen in his letters to Bertrand Russell around the year 1915, where he voices his opposition to enfranchising the working class and his hostility to the burgeoning labour movements, and disparages the French Revolution, referring to "Liberty, Equality, and Fraternity" as the "three-fanged serpent". Rather than a republic, Lawrence called for an absolute dictator and equivalent dictatrix to lord over the lower peoples. Earlier, Harrison had drawn attention to the vein of sadism that runs through Lawrence's writing.

Lawrence held seemingly contradictory views on feminism. The evidence of his written works, particularly his earlier novels, indicates an overwhelming commitment to representing women as strong, independent and complex ; as noted above he produced major works in which young, self-directing female characters were central. In his youth he supported extending the vote to women, and once wrote, "All women in their natures are like giantesses. They will break through everything and go on with their own lives." However, a number of feminist critics, notably Kate Millett, have criticised, indeed ridiculed Lawrence's sexual politics, Millett claiming that he uses his female characters as mouthpieces to promote his creed of male supremacy, and that his story The Woman Who Rode Away showed Lawrence as a pornographic sadist with its portrayal of "human sacrifice performed upon the woman to the greater glory and potency of the male." Brenda Maddox further highlights this story and two others written around the same time, St. Mawr and The Princess, as "masterworks of misogyny".

Despite the inconsistency and at times inscrutability of his philosophical writings Lawrence continues to find an audience, and the ongoing publication of a new scholarly edition of his letters and writings has demonstrated the range of his achievement. Philosophers like Gilles Deleuze and Félix Guattari found in Lawrence's critique of Freud an important precursor of anti-Oedipal accounts of the unconscious that has been much influential.

Written works

Novels

Lawrence is best known for his novels Sons and Lovers, The Rainbow, Women in Love and Lady Chatterley's Lover. In these books, Lawrence explores the possibilities for life within an industrial setting. In particular Lawrence is concerned with the nature of relationships that can be had within such a setting. Though often classed as a realist, Lawrence in fact uses his characters to give form to his personal philosophy. His depiction of sexuality, though seen as shocking when his work was first published in the early 20th century, has its roots in this highly personal way of thinking and being.

It is worth noting that Lawrence was very interested in the sense of touch and that his focus on physical intimacy has its roots in a desire to restore an emphasis on the body, and re-balance it with what he perceived to be Western civilisation's over-emphasis on the mind; writing in a 1929 essay "Men Must Work and Women As Well", he stated,

> "Now we see the trend of our civilization, in terms of human feeling and human relation. It is, and there is no denying it, towards a greater and greater abstraction from the physical, towards a further and further physical separateness between men and women, and between individual and individual... It only remains for some men and women, individuals, to try to get back their bodies and preserve the flow of warmth, affection and physical unison." Phoenix II : Uncollected Writings, Ed. Warren Roberts and Harry T. Moore (New York) 1970

In his later years Lawrence developed the potentialities of the short novel form in St Mawr, The Virgin and the Gypsy and The Escaped Cock.

Short stories

Lawrence's best-known short stories include "The Captain's Doll", "The Fox", "The Ladybird", "Odour of Chrysanthemums", "The Princess", "The Rocking-Horse Winner", "St Mawr", "The Virgin and the Gypsy" and "The Woman who Rode Away". (The Virgin and the Gypsy was published as a novella after he died.) Among his most praised collections is The Prussian Officer and Other Stories, published in 1914. His collection The Woman Who Rode Away and Other Stories, published in 1928, develops the theme of leadership that Lawrence also explored in novels such as Kangaroo, The Plumed Serpent and Fanny and Annie.

Poetry

Although best known for his novels, Lawrence wrote almost 800 poems, most of them relatively short. His first poems were written in 1904 and two of his poems, "Dreams Old" and "Dreams Nascent", were among his earliest published works in The English Review. It has been claimed that his early works clearly place him in the school of Georgian poets, and indeed some of his poems appear in the Georgian Poetry anthologies. However, James Reeves in his book on Georgian Poetry, notes that Lawrence was never really a Georgian poet. Indeed, later critics contast Lawrence's energy and dynamism with the complacency of Georgian poetry.

Just as the First World War dramatically changed the work of many of the poets who saw service in the trenches, Lawrence's own work saw a dramatic change, during his years in Cornwall. During this time, he wrote free verse influenced by Walt Whitman. He set forth his manifesto for much of his later verse in the introduction to New Poems. "We can get rid of the stereotyped movements and the old hackneyed associations of sound or sense. We can break down those artificial conduits and canals through which we do so love to force our utterance. We can break the stiff neck of habit ... But we cannot positively prescribe any motion, any rhythm."

Lawrence rewrote many of his novels several times to perfect them and similarly he returned to some of his early poems when they were collected in 1928. This was in part to fictionalise them, but also to remove some of the artifice of his first works. As he put in himself : "A young man is afraid of his demon and puts his hand over the demon's mouth sometimes and speaks for him." His best-known poems are probably those dealing with nature such as those in the collection Birds, Beasts and Flowers, including the Tortoise poems, and "Snake", one of his most frequently anthologised, displays some of his most frequent concerns: those of man's modern distance from nature and subtle hints at religious themes.

> In the deep, strange-scented shade of the great dark carob tree
> I came down the steps with my pitcher
> And must wait, must stand and wait, for there he was at the trough before me.
> (From "Snake")

Look ! We have come through ! is his other work from the period of the end of the war and it reveals another important element common to much of his writings ; his inclination to lay himself bare in his writings. Although Lawrence could be regarded as a writer of love poems, his usually deal in the less romantic aspects of love such as sexual frustration or the sex act itself. Ezra Pound in his Literary Essays complained of Lawrence's interest in his own "disagreeable sensations" but praised him for his "low-life narrative." This is a reference to Lawrence's dialect poems akin to the Scots poems of Robert Burns, in which he reproduced the language and concerns of the people of Nottinghamshire from his youth.

> Tha thought tha wanted ter be rid o' me.
> 'Appen tha did, an' a'.
> Tha thought tha wanted ter marry an' se

If ter couldna be master an' th' woman's boss,
Tha'd need a woman different from me,
An' tha knowed it; ay, yet tha comes across
Ter say goodbye! an' a'.
(From "The Drained Cup")

Although Lawrence's works after his Georgian period are clearly in the modernist tradition, they were often very different from those of many other modernist writers, such as Pound. Pound's poems were often austere, with every word carefully worked on. Lawrence felt all poems had to be personal sentiments, and that a sense of spontaneity was vital. He called one collection of poems Pansies, partly for the simple ephemeral nature of the verse, but also as a pun on the French word panser, to dress or bandage a wound. "Pansies", as he made explicit in the introduction to New Poems, is also a pun on Blaise Pascal's Pensées. "The Noble Englishman" and "Don't Look at Me" were removed from the official edition of Pansies on the grounds of obscenity, which wounded him. Even though he lived most of the last ten years of his life abroad, his thoughts were often still on England.

O the stale old dogs who pretend to guard
the morals of the masses,
how smelly they make the great back-yard
wetting after everyone that passes.
(From "The Young and Their Moral Guardians")

Two notebooks of Lawrence's unprinted verse were posthumously published as Last Poems and More Pansies. These contain two of Lawrence's most famous poems about death, "Bavarian Gentians" and "The Ship of Death".

Literary criticism

Lawrence's criticism of other authors often provides insight into his own thinking and writing. Of particular note is his Study of Thomas Hardy and Other Essays. In Studies in Classic American Literature Lawrence's responses to writers like Walt Whitman, Herman Melville and Edgar Allan Poe also shed light on his craft.

Painting

D. H. Lawrence had a lifelong interest in painting, which became one of his main forms of expression in his last years. His paintings were exhibited at the Warren Gallery in London's Mayfair in 1929. The exhibition was extremely controversial, with many of the 13,000 people visiting mainly to gawk. The Daily Express claimed, "Fight with an Amazon represents a hideous, bearded man holding a fair-haired woman in his lascivious grip while wolves with dripping jaws look on expectantly, [this] is frankly indecent". However, several artists and art experts praised the paintings. Gwen John, reviewing the exhibition in Everyman, spoke of Lawrence's "stupendous gift of self-expression" and singled out The Finding of Moses, Red Willow Trees and Boccaccio Story as "pictures of real beauty and great vitality". Others singled out Contadini for special praise. After a complaint, the police seized thirteen of the twenty-five paintings (including Boccaccio Story and Contadini). Despite declarations of support from many writers, artists and Members of Parliament, Lawrence was able to recover his paintings only by agreeing never to exhibit them in England again. The largest collection of the paintings is now at La Fonda de Taos hotel in Taos, New Mexico. Several others, including Boccaccio Storyand Resurrection, are at the Humanities Research Centre of the University of Texas at Austin.

Lady Chatterley trial

A heavily censored abridgement of Lady Chatterley's Lover was published in the United States by Alfred A. Knopf in 1928. This edition was posthumously re-issued in paperback there both by Signet Books and by Penguin Books in 1946 When the full unexpurgated edition of Lady Chatterley's Lover was published by Penguin Books in Britain in 1960, the trial of Penguin under the Obscene Publications Act of 1959 became a major public event and a test of the new obscenity law. The 1959 act (introduced by Roy Jenkins) had made it possible for publishers to escape conviction if they could show that a work was of literary merit. One of the objections was to the frequent use of the word "fuck" and its derivatives and the word "cunt".

Various academic critics and experts of diverse kinds, including E. M. Forster, Helen Gardner, Richard Hoggart, Raymond Williams and Norman St John-Stevas, were called as witnesses, and the verdict, delivered on 2 November 1960, was "not guilty". This resulted in a far greater degree of freedom for publishing explicit material in the UK. The prosecution was ridiculed for being out of touch with changing social norms when the chief prosecutor, Mervyn Griffith-Jones, asked if it were the kind of book "you would wish your wife or servants to read".

The Penguin second edition, published in 1961, contains a publisher's dedication, which reads: "For having published this book, Penguin Books were prosecuted under the Obscene Publications Act, 1959 at the Old Bailey in London from 20 October to 2 November 1960. This edition is therefore dedicated to the twelve jurors, three women and nine men, who returned a verdict of 'Not Guilty' and thus made D. H. Lawrence's last novel available for the first time to the public in the United Kingdom."

Posthumous reputation

The obituaries shortly after Lawrence's death were, with the exception of the one by E. M. Forster, unsympathetic or hostile. However, there were those who articulated a more favourable recognition of the significance of this author's life and works. For example, his long-time friend Catherine Carswell summed up his life in a letter to the periodical Time and Tide published on 16 March 1930. In response to his critics, she claimed:

> "In the face of formidable initial disadvantages and lifelong delicacy, poverty that lasted for three quarters of his life and hostility that survives his death, he did nothing that he did not really want to do, and all that he most wanted to do he did. He went all over the world, he owned a ranch, he lived in the most beautiful corners of Europe, and met whom he wanted to meet and told them that they were wrong and he was right. He painted and made things, and sang, and rode. He wrote something like three dozen books, of which even the worst page dances with life that could be mistaken for no other man's, while the best are admitted, even by those who hate him, to be unsurpassed. Without vices, with most human virtues, the husband of one wife, scrupulously honest, this estimable citizen yet managed to keep free from the shackles of civilization and the cant of literary cliques. He would have laughed

lightly and cursed venomously in passing at the solemn owls—each one secretly chained by the leg—who now conduct his inquest. To do his work and lead his life in spite of them took some doing, but he did it, and long after they are forgotten, sensitive and innocent people—if any are left—will turn Lawrence's pages and will know from them what sort of a rare man Lawrence was."

Aldous Huxley also defended Lawrence in his introduction to a collection of letters published in 1932. However, the most influential advocate of Lawrence's literary reputation was Cambridge literary critic F. R. Leavis, who asserted that the author had made an important contribution to the tradition of English fiction. Leavis stressed that The Rainbow, Women in Love, and the short stories and tales were major works of art. Later, the obscenity trials over the unexpurgated edition of Lady Chatterley's Lover in America in 1959, and in Britain in 1960, and subsequent publication of the full text, ensured Lawrence's popularity (and notoriety) with a wider public.

Since 2008, an annual D. H. Lawrence Festival has been organised in Eastwood to celebrate Lawrence's life and works; in September 2016, events were held in Cornwall to celebrate the centenary of Lawrence's connection with Zennor.

Selected depictions of Lawrence's life

- Priest of Love: a 1981 film based on the non-fiction biography of Lawrence of the same name. It starred Ian McKellen as Lawrence. The film is mostly focused on Lawrence's time in Taos, New Mexico, and Italy, although the source biography covers most of his life.
- Coming Through: a 1985 film about Lawrence who is portrayed by Kenneth Branagh.
- Zennor in Darkness, a 1993 novel by Helen Dunmore in which Lawrence and his wife feature prominently.
- Look ! We Have Come Through ! : a stage play based on the letters and works of Lawrence and his wife, Frieda. Scripted by James Petosa and Carole Graham Lehan. Nominated for the Helen Hayes Award, 1998.
- On the Rocks: a 2008 stage play by Amy Rosenthal showing Lawrence, Frieda Lawrence, Mansfield and Murry in Cornwall in 1916–17.
- LAWRENCE – Scandalous ! Censored ! Banned ! : A musical based on the life of Lawrence. Winner of the 2009 Marquee Theatre Award for Best Original Musical. Received its London Premiere in October 2013 at the Bridewell Theatre.
- Husbands and Sons: A stage play based on Lawrence's stories of growing up in a mining community and brought to the Royal Court Theatre in London by Peter Gill in 1968 and revived at the National Theatre in London in 2015.

Works

Novels

- The White Peacock (1911)
- The Trespasser (1912)
- Sons and Lovers (1913)
- The Rainbow (1915)
- Women in Love (1920)
- The Lost Girl (1920)
- Aaron's Rod (1922)
- Kangaroo (1923)
- The Boy in the Bush (1924)
- The Plumed Serpent (1926)
- Lady Chatterley's Lover (1928)
- The Escaped Cock (1929), later re-published as The Man Who Died

Short stories collections

- The Prussian Officer and Other Stories (1914)
- England, My England and Other Stories (1922)
- The Horse Dealer's Daughter (1922)
- The Fox, The Captain's Doll, The Ladybird (1923)
- St Mawr and other stories (1925)
- The Woman who Rode Away and other stories (1928)
- The Rocking-Horse Winner (1926)
- Mother and Daughter (1929)
- The Virgin and the Gipsy and Other Stories (1930)
- Love Among the Haystacks and other stories (1930)
- Collected Stories (1994) – Everyman's Library

Collected letters

- The Letters of D. H. Lawrence, Volume I, September 1901 – May 1913, ed. James T. Boulton, Cambridge University Press, 1979, ISBN 0-521-22147-1
- The Letters of D. H. Lawrence, Volume II, June 1913 – October 1916, ed. George J. Zytaruk and James T. Boulton, Cambridge University Press, 1981, ISBN 0-521-23111-6
- The Letters of D. H. Lawrence, Volume III, October 1916 – June 1921, ed. James T. Boulton and Andrew Robertson, Cambridge University Press, 1984, ISBN 0-521-23112-4
- The Letters of D. H. Lawrence, Volume IV, June 1921 – March 1924 , ed. Warren Roberts, James T. Boulton and Elizabeth Mansfield, Cambridge University Press, 1987, ISBN 0-521-00695-3
- The Letters of D. H. Lawrence, Volume V, March 1924 – March 1927, ed. James T. Boulton and Lindeth Vasey, Cambridge University Press, 1989, ISBN 0-521-00696-1
- The Letters of D. H. Lawrence, Volume VI, March 1927 – November 1928 , ed. James T. Boulton and Margaret Boulton with Gerald M. Lacy, Cambridge University Press, 1991, ISBN 0-521-00698-8
- The Letters of D. H. Lawrence, Volume VII, November 1928 – February 1930, ed. Keith Sagar and James T. Boulton, Cambridge University Press, 1993, ISBN 0-521-00699-6
- The Letters of D. H. Lawrence, with index, Volume VIII, ed. James T. Boulton, Cambridge University Press, 2001, ISBN 0-521-23117-5
- The Selected Letters of D H Lawrence, Compiled and edited by James T. Boulton, Cambridge University Press, 1997, ISBN 0-521-40115-1

Poetry collections

- Love Poems and others (1913)
- Amores (1916)
- Look ! We have come through ! (1917)
- New Poems (1918)
- Bay : a book of poems (1919)
- Tortoises (1921)
- Birds, Beasts and Flowers (1923)
- The Collected Poems of D H Lawrence (1928)
- Pansies (1929)
- Nettles (1930)
- Last Poems (1932)
- Fire and other poems (1940)
- The Complete Poems of D H Lawrence (1964), ed. Vivian de Sola Pinto and F. Warren Roberts
- The White Horse (1964)
- D. H. Lawrence : Selected Poems (1972), ed. Keith Sagar.

Plays

- The Daughter-in-Law (1912)
- The Widowing of Mrs Holroyd (1914)
- Touch and Go (1920)
- David (1926)
- The Fight for Barbara (1933)
- A Collier's Friday Night (1934)
- The Married Man (1940)
- The Merry-Go-Round (1941)
- The Complete Plays of D H Lawrence (1965)
- The Plays, edited by Hans-Wilhelm Schwarze and John Worthen, Cambridge University Press, 1999, ISBN 0-521-24277-0

Non-fiction books and pamphlets

- Study of Thomas Hardy and other essays (1914), edited by Bruce Steele, Cambridge University Press, 1985, ISBN 0-521-25252-0, Literary criticism and metaphysics
- Movements in European History (1921), edited by Philip Crumpton, Cambridge University Press, 1989, ISBN 0-521-26201-1, Originally published under the name of Lawrence H. Davison
- Psychoanalysis and the Unconscious and Fantasia of the Unconscious (1921/1922), edited by Bruce Steele, Cambridge University Press, 2004 ISBN 0-521-32791-1
- Studies in Classic American Literature (1923), edited by Ezra Greenspan, Lindeth Vasey and John Worthen, Cambridge University Press, 2003, ISBN 0-521-55016-5
- Reflections on the Death of a Porcupine and other essays (1925), edited by Michael Herbert, Cambridge University Press, 1988, ISBN 0-521-26622-X
- A Propos of Lady Chatterley's Lover (1929) – Lawrence wrote this pamphlet to explain his novel
- Apocalypse and the writings on Revelation (1931) edited by Mara Kalnins, Cambridge University Press, 1980, ISBN 0-521-22407-1
- Phoenix: The Posthumous Papers of D. H. Lawrence (1936)
- Phoenix II: Uncollected, Unpublished and Other Prose Works by D. H. Lawrence (1968)
- Introductions and Reviews, edited by N. H. Reeve and John Worthen, Cambridge University Press, 2004, ISBN 0-521-83584-4
- Late Essays and Articles, edited by James T. Boulton, Cambridge University Press, 2004, ISBN 0-521-58431-0
- Selected Letters, Oneworld Classics, 2008. Edited by James T. Boulton. ISBN 978-1-84749-049-0

Travel books

- Twilight in Italy and Other Essays (1916), edited by Paul Eggert, Cambridge University Press, 1994, ISBN 0-521-26888-5. Twilight in Italy paperback reissue, I.B.Tauris, 2015, ISBN 978-1-78076-965-3
- Sea and Sardinia (1921), edited by Mara Kalnins, Cambridge University Press, 1997, ISBN 0-521-24275-4
- Mornings in Mexico and Other Essays (1927), edited by Virginia Crosswhite Hyde, Cambridge University Press, 2009, ISBN 978-0-521-65292-6.
- Sketches of Etruscan Places and other Italian essays (1932), edited by Simonetta de Filippis, Cambridge University Press, 1992, ISBN 0-521-25253-9

Works translated by Lawrence

- Lev Isaakovich Shestov All Things are Possible (1920)
- Ivan Alekseyevich Bunin The Gentleman from San Francisco (1922), tr. with S. S. Koteliansky
- Giovanni Verga Mastro-Don Gesualdo (1923)
- Giovanni Verga Little Novels of Sicily (1925)
- Giovanni Verga Cavalleria Rusticana and other stories (1928)
- Antonio Francesco Grazzini The Story of Doctor Manente (1929)

Manuscripts and early drafts of published novels and other works

- Paul Morel (1911–12), edited by Helen Baron, Cambridge University Press, 2003, ISBN 0-521-56009-8, an early manuscript version of Sons and Lovers
- The First Women in Love (1916–17) edited by John Worthen and Lindeth Vasey, Cambridge University Press, 1998, ISBN 0-521-37326-3
- Mr Noon, (unfinished novel) Parts I and II, edited by Lindeth Vasey, Cambridge University Press, 1984, ISBN 0-521-25251-2
- The Symbolic Meaning : The Uncollected Versions of Studies in Classic American Literature, edited by Armin Arnold, Centaur Press, 1962
- Quetzalcoatl (1925), edited by Louis L Martz, W W Norton Edition, 1998, ISBN 0-8112-1385-4, Early draft of The Plumed Serpent
- The First and Second Lady Chatterley novels, edited by Dieter Mehl and Christa Jansohn, Cambridge University Press, 1999, ISBN 0-521-47116-8.

Paintings

- The Paintings of D. H. Lawrence, London : Mandrake Press, 1929.
- D. H. Lawrence's Paintings, ed. Keith Sagar, London : Chaucer Press, 2003.
- The Collected Art Works of D. H. Lawrence, ed. Tetsuji Kohno, Tokyo : Sogensha, 2004.

L.&.D
edition

CPSIA information can be obtained
at www.ICGtesting.com
Printed in the USA
LVHW050724290820
664472LV00013B/1464

9 781728 911779